*For all the Jabaris, young and old, in name and in spirit—*
*some of whom I've been lucky enough to connect with personally.*
*And for my cousins, who will be practically*
*grown by the time they read this: first there was Dantae*
*and then, quickly after, Aedan.*

This book was typeset in Lora. The illustrations were done in pencil, watercolor, and collage, then colored digitally.
Candlewick Press, 99 Dover Street, Somerville, Massachusetts 02144. www.candlewick.com.
Printed in Humen, Dongguan, China. 20 21 22 23 24 25 APS 10 9 8 7 6 5 4 3 2 1

# JABARI TRIES

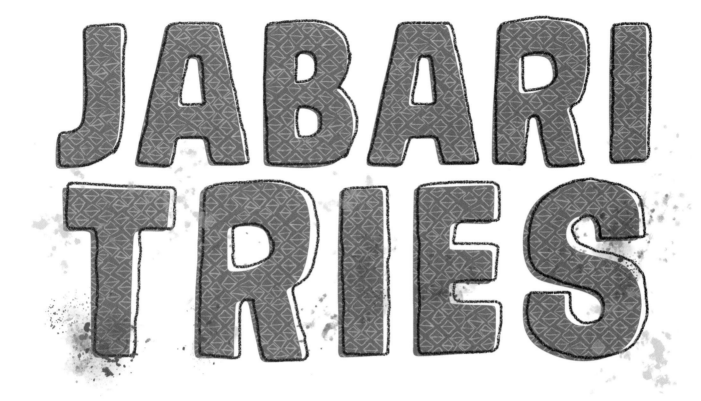

Gaia Cornwall

CANDLEWICK PRESS

"I'm making a flying machine today!" Jabari told his dad.

"Wow," said his dad.

"Me!" said Nika.

"My machine will fly all the way across the yard!" said Jabari.
"It'll be easy—I don't need any help!"

Jabari built an excellent ramp.
He put his flying machine at the very top.

Whoosh, AROUND, AROUND,

up it went! And C R A S H

His machine did not fly.
"Maybe it's too heavy," said Jabari.

"Me!" said Nika.

"Not now, Nika," said Jabari. "I am concentrating. I need something to make my machine go up."

He thought about how inventors have to use their creativity and how engineers and scientists work to solve problems.

Lewis Howard Latimer

Dr. Flossie Wong-Staal

Roy Allela

Dr. Shirley Ann Jackson

Jabari gathered up all his tools. He prepared his space.

He sketched and planned.

"I think the ramp has to be big," Jabari said. "Really big."

After a lot of building and stacking and hammering and sticking, Jabari was ready.

Zip, flip,

"Me!" said Nika.

"Nika, don't! You'll break it!"

swoosh around, up,

SMASH!

"You know, I bet Nika would love to help out," said his dad. Jabari looked at Nika.

"I don't need any help," he said.

"What if you thought of her more like a partner?" said his dad. "Lots of great inventors have had partners."

"Me!" said Nika.

"We'll try it out," said Jabari.

"Maybe we need more power, Nika," said Jabari.

The engineers measured and mixed.

"Me?" said Nika.

Jabari handed his partner a stirring tool.

Trickle, pour,

twist, turn,

bubble, pop, fiiiiizzzz . . .

POW!

BASH

"Nothing is working!"

His chest felt tight, and his neck felt like a sunburn.

Jabari wanted to cry.

He took a tiny rest.

"Hey," said his dad, "I see you're really upset."

"I'm frustrated," said Jabari.

"It looks like a frustrating problem," said his dad. "When I'm frustrated, I gather up all my patience, take a deep breath, and blow away all the mixed feelings inside."

"And then you try again?" said Jabari.

"And then I try again," said his dad.

Jabari gathered up all his patience. He closed his eyes and took a deep breath. He blew away all his muddy feelings. He felt his body calm down. He felt his brain starting to work better.

Nika squeezed his hand.

"Let's try again," said Jabari.

The partners thought and thought together.

"Me," said Nika.

"That's it, Nika!" said Jabari. "Maybe we need better wings!"

They cut and glued and shaped and tied.

*Tinker, twist, snap, snip!*

Nika found the launch spot. Jabari held the
flying machine up, pulled back, and . . .

# whoosh, UP,

"Wheeeee!" said Nika.

flying!

"You did it!" said his dad.

"We did it!" said Jabari. "It went all the way across the yard! We're great engineers!"

"We!" said Nika.

"And guess what?"

"What?" said his dad.

"Rocket to Jupiter is next!"
"Me!" said Nika.